CU01510009

Praise for Gardner Dorton & If I Were God I Would Also Start With Light

∂

"Gardner Dorton's *If I Were a God I Would Also Start With Light* actually springs forth from darkness; the gloom of being queer within a hostile family and community. We see how familial and religious trauma disrupt queer desire and limit later opportunities for love, acceptance, and joy. The speaker of these poems undertakes the sizable quest of finding alternative role models in order to reconstruct the desire that has been long denied. Dorton turns our heads towards art, drops us into the eye of the storm as his speaker navigates mental illness, and suspends us in moments equally jarring and intimate to illustrate that the journey to "sheer, queer joy" requires resilience, a different kind of faith than the one we are taught."

—Taylor Byas, author of *I Done Clicked My Heels Three Times*

"In *If I Were God I Would Also Start With Light*, Dorton redefines divinity. With radiant language and unabashed queerness, this powerful new collection navigates religion, identity, and longing with an intimate and heart-wrenching beauty, brimming with poems that are "eager and crowded with life." Dorton has gifted us with a new kind of holy book and I, for one, am all in."

—Adam Gianforcaro, author of *Every Living Day*

∂

"Gardner Dorton's collection of poems *If I Were God I Would Also Start With Light* is a first baptism where we are reminded that there is "phlegm and violence in every prayer." Dorton is grabbing our hand and guiding us through the church, through the field, through the "hollow landscapes," through all the places queerness lives in danger. There is so much space in between each poem, room for us to walk around and grow, to turn away from the trauma of both God and family in order to learn how to love. This collection teaches us how to sing through our sadness; that there might always be something worth praying to, often it is not God but love itself."

—Jason B. Crawford, author of *YEET!* & *Year of the Unicorn Kidz*

"*If I Were God I Would Also Start With Light* is a debut collection that knows what it means to stay tender—despite God's wrath, despite God-wind, despite God-fearing men (with their heavy hands and their picket signs). Twining religion with natural wonder and Southern topography, Gardner Dorton speaks clearly: "I apologize for adding more mysticism to this / world, but I've realized that this is how it all came to be." Here, you'll find poems steadfast in their joy and meticulous in cataloging the contents of their hearts—from outside the Ark to Virginia fields, from eating over the trashcan to your local Target—here are poems: "a prairie, eager and crowded with life." If I Were God I Would Also Start With Light is a gift, and much like light itself, dazzling in its brilliance."

—Ashley Cline, author of *to eat the sleeping sky, whole*

∂

"In Gardner Dorton's sublime, Appalachian debut, a modern oracle speaks from the desert of grief, boyhood, and violence. In sharp, precise language drawing from scripture and from place, Dorton asserts the importance of a single question, of small miracles. The importance of seeing then waiting. Like Jericho marching around the city walls in defiance or Job abiding in his dejection from God, Dorton speaks to the power of transfiguration through the erotic, through self determination, and through queer self actualization. Here, one finds wings among the carnage and emerges with a new, vibrant, whole-life, a "second / chance" of grace and redemption. This is a haunting collection from a memorable new voice."

—Halle Hill, author of *Good Women: Stories*

"Dorton's poetry is courageous as much as it is emotional. In this collection, a gentle soul fights for survival, and along the way has picked up a remarkable gift of poetry to protect himself. His writing braves the fearful darkness of life, and hands life back over to us, still raw, yet somehow undeniably beautiful, a miracle in language."

—Nicholas Goodly, author of *Black Swim*

"At the border of death and resurrection, *If I Were God I Would Also Start With Light* is a collection of poems from exile. Dorton's words sound with the force of a prophet preaching in the wilderness. Urgent, hungry—his message is ultimately one of queer self-determination. Crows, flies, bruises, and ash populate this landscape, but so do pearls, light, fruit, and dogwood blossoms. Dorton writes, "There still is / grief in the garden." Like a drunken voicemail left for God, these poems are unsparingly honest. They take inventory of suffering alongside joy and are not afraid to confront or invent. In response to a Baptist church questionnaire and a triage intake form, Dorton asks questions. What does it mean to be a body? What does it mean to hold what you've been given, whether or not you wanted it? What does it mean to keep living? "If this is the end, / or close to it, it was an honor to eat / everything this world had to offer." For all the places this book takes us, it leaves me with hope. This book is a gift."

—Joshua Garcia, author of *Pentimento*

If I Were God
I Would Also
Start With Light

poems

Gardner Dorton

Thirty West Publishing House

ISBN-13: 979-8-9895422-6-0

Edited by Olivia Zarzycki

Cover art and design by Knox Peters

Printed in the U.S.A.

For more titles and inquiries, please visit:

www.thirtywestph.com

For sheer, queer joy

Table of Contents

And Jesus said to them,
"A prophet is not without honor,
except in his hometown and among
his relatives and in his own household."

—Mark 6:4 (English Standard Version)

If I Were God I Would Also Start With Light

∂

Baptism Questionnaire

(Questions selected from a
Baptist church questionnaire.)

*Tell us about your life prior to coming to faith in Christ.
For example, you may share about your family background,
religious experiences you had growing up, or how you
conceived of God before becoming a Christian:*

Once, my grandfather pulled a hook
from the bleeding lip of a fish
and told me what men do to women:

catch and release, sometimes eat.

I am a boy clichéd by melancholia,
who has made a grocery list of only bleach.
I make happy homes with my hands
and flatten them. Undefined,
sneaking glances at the nave
of other boys' necks. A wind chimes out
of key. Father, heavenly father,
what bait was I given?

Have you been excommunicated from another local church? If
so, please explain the circumstances:

Here is a stack of cease-and-desist letters.
Here are the petitions nailed by train spikes to my door.
Here, the lamb blood threats painted on the frame.
Here are the letters signed with a bullseye.
Here, slurs thrown from moving vehicles. Here, take them.

How has your life changed since coming to faith in Christ?
Where do you see evidence of God's grace at work in your
life?:

What if I am still afraid of men?
The man unloading the clip of his gun
at the moon because it looks like his mother.
The one who pulled out his penis and asked
remember it? The one covered in his own blood.
The scores of them I've loved mercilessly.
The plumb eaters, ass-gropers, and global deciders.
The church chorus singers and priests holding back the neck
of an animal. The mountain-top
messiahs transfiguring behind a beach towel.
The one putting a kitchen knife
to my forearms. The familial one.

Were you baptized by immersion in water after your
conversion to Christ?:

What happens when the water
overflows the reeds on the river bank?
The mountains swallow back
their lost granite and shale.

There are marks on my body
that I didn't leave, is that
a miracle? There are bruises
the size of irregular fruit, is that?
What is hell? Did you make it?
I dipped a godhead into wax
and kept it bedside—a blaspheme?

What if I come up from the water
and my tongue falls through
a new hole in my chin? Am I
the miracle—my body escaping
itself from every direction?

Please explain the Gospel. Write it out as you would share it
with a non-Christian friend:

It's an escort of giants. Of booming
footsteps. A hell pit where my booze-
soaked pores burn easier. A *fag-spit spinning*
feast over the fire—you told me that.

It's the exposure of every recipe I wrote
down in hunger. The litany of high school
secrets, am I getting closer to correct?

Okay, it's the cannibal twin I absorbed eating
his way out. The other one who should have,
taking his turn. The life, the second
chance and the swallowing. That's it.

No, it's—

1.

Polaroid

after *Three Boys,* a painting by Salmon Toor

You're slacked over
and feathered in your own
brilliance, and my grip on your
figure is loosening.
And there's me, the curly-haired
farm boy, your boy.
You bite my pierced ear
and it falls off like a pear halve.
I promise no redemption.
I promise no drop of water
for your parched tongue, not even
the sweat rung from my button-up.
I am a pool of non-excellence.
I am the border of your photograph.

Townsend

Do not stand so far away from your art, judging it,
like a believer. To fear how far you will fall is a learned
behavior, to relish the sensation is a perversion that I love
you for. Find angels and floaters. These mountains are a holy
war. Quietly, the devil is whispering through
the sycamores making bad gospels, making worse
omens. Fog pillars dominoing over by Appalachian wind.
I apologize for adding more mysticism to this
world, but I've realized that this is how it all came to be.

Heartbreak//Hercules's Eleventh Labor

Your Mouth, a frown's length, is spilling
with words that fill every fracture.

Into water, I was born from tongues
with mythology written by itself,

I've seen this before, the filibuster, or
when I walk away cup-handed after

Self-fulfilling prophecy where I lose.
The stout arm overturns

stripping away my roots, the ground
advising to get my feet back.

me below the sky, but above my mother,
to the place my secret is buried.

I'm asking for a miracle, Love,
with a bottle in my hand.

In front of a counsel of titans,
there is no miracle I can ask for,

The glass erupted when I gripped
strong enough to prove I could.

this man of god, looking for a fight,
he then read the fortune on my palms.

Hypomania

I'm Invincible.
Say I'm invincible
or prove otherwise.

True shock only comes
from looking down at your hands
and finding them there.

I'm still there. A tall stone.

I'm tireless of cruelty,
of enacting it on myself.
The right stone, a fist,
cast first.

I can outrun it, I can move
at the speed of failed stillness.
I could panic less if I moved more.

I'm a disaster of paperwork.
Look, my hands are still
here—still laughing.

God-Wind

I'm finally leaving
Hell. My voice is brass, church
bells knocking an epidemic
of insight. I woke up
on the summit with wind
licking my hair perfect,
my feet already on
the ground. I understand how
someone could believe gods lived here.
Everywhere I look I see
emblazoned sublimity, light
that looks better through glass, spirits
crawling out the rafters. I have vision.
I have visions. I won't tell you
what they are.

A Man Walks Into a Bar and Disassociates

After Shoe Theory by Richard Siken

A man walks in only his skin in the park.
It's freezing in devil's hour. He has
your hands. He has the rest of you, too.
Call him yourself.

A man didn't sleep well again last night. Instead,
he snapped sunflower seeds without eating them.
He went downtown to watch the sunrise.
He'd seen better.

A man, same one, yourself, is trying to stay
alive. *No man is an ocean*, he quotes incorrectly.
He's the small boat banging the cliff-side
on the island. He's a jumper. He's a freefall.

A man can no longer speak, bankrupt
of language. He uses whatever sticks
he can gather from the forest floor to make words.
He turns primal. He turns to where
his god should be. He listens closely and finds
that he is not the only one tongue-tied.

You Will Never/Always Be Alone

Once I was searching for the love of my life
over a seascape crashing cymbals against the rock face,

washed in gray air. I thought I saw him swimming
towards the cliff, but it was just huddled

discard: diet soda bottles and synthetic boas, a neighborhood
of plankton and small life. Go looking and you will find

something. And so, I was several decades (a perfect vision
diced in static) and this I do alone. I'm careful what I desire.

I daydream about phantoms, walking my dog along the ridge
beside the wheat and wildflowers. They say *a prophet*

is never loved in his hometown, but I'll tell you, it's more
a prophet is never loved. It's about turning light

with your hands, letting shapes reveal themselves
while something darts towards you in the water.

When you're ready for it.

MEARCSTAPA.

I am coming home, The Line-Walker,
who walks between up and down, heaven

and ground. Because here, *ethereal*
means lonely and *star-lit* means

dark. I am no closer to God the way
a bridge is no closer to either side.

I am falling unburdened, Babel returning
to origin and singularity—at peace

to be back in place. I will find
a resting spot, one plop into the ocean

when my wings have burned off.

My First Baptism

was by spit. The angel's foot
on my neck and your grizzly hand
on my sternum. I am trying to speak
like the many-eyed angels,
phlegm and violence in every prayer.
I swallow spit and your sweat becomes
brilliant jewels on your New King James Bible.
I hate you. You tell me God hates
those who know too little
about him. I am saved
on stained concrete in a strip
mall church. I reach for heaven
and you grab my mouth, squeeze
an "O" from my lips until
my Accutane face bleeds a snake
of blood. You tell me I am blessed,
that I will learn virtue.
I am unlearned and drying out.
You give me a water bottle
and say you remade me.
I finally understand that grief
was always outside the garden.

Anthropocene

It may be time to go back
to the old gods. Hermes purses
his lips and pulls an asphodel from them,
already on fire. & I see a church
in his newly cupped hands.
So now I am an oracle for the final
age. I haven't slept in 36 hours
& everything looks like my grandfather's
hands—two unholy burning stones.
I've known catharsis under many names,
& tonight it is my swollen right eye,
violet and violent at 3 am, a personal trope.
When we talk about wrath, we are not
talking about an atom bomb, but the bleat
of another post-midnight soul.
A child away from his parents,
and a man with cigar breath doing
what men do. I don't mean to diminish
anyone's suffering. When I say
I've seen a man die, what I mean
is many and always. So, I die
over and over, and my queer fathers wait
on me as leather effigies on the edge
of their seats. See, I am a part of a country
that only survives by dropping
hot suns over everywhere else.
My country, save me from Hermes'
bouquet. The final age of driving
the golden spike between
our split jaw and banded earth.
I wanted to write an aubade,
but who has the time to wake so slowly?

Disassociation in Your Local Target

I rang your phone
I rang the bells
so loudly hell
has been up
for hours don't
start a sentence
without knowing
all the ways it
will misfire I rang
your phone and got
lost trying
to make new
idioms I'm such an
idiot the stove
set to low
for hours puffing
like incense
sometimes I suffer
just to have more
to confess I cried
for hours when
they drove
the neighbor off
from across
the street some deaths
you feel invasive
for mourning but I'm
being too hard on
myself again I RANG
YOUR PHONE and wrung
myself out like a rind
on the rim of a glass
filled with morning-time
anxiety this is the part
of the song I always
forget but where
I dance the hardest

Cicada-Man

Have you also seen the human
        in Van Gogh's *Three Cicadas*? Look
at the hooks of their legs, in how they make
        parentheses.

(Like his shoulders are sketched right into it.)

I am not the kind to bury something
        twice. Or the kind to hear
voices from dark corners.

I don't shed like the cicada—
        loudly.

(This may all be a lie.)

Some things live in the unsettling between
        hell and earth. Come, disappear and come
again, like how a tombstone is only half buried.

I buried him once, smirking under black funeral
        garb. The bugs in the trees wailing their skin off.

Aristotle named the cicada
        a symbol of immortality and resurrection.

(I must agree, a man still walking.)

Failed Elegy

a ballista in a pottery shop
a bag of broken china rattling in the doorway
a melted doll, droopy-lipped and sarcastic
a dirge
a hen
a cock
their drumsticks
a hospital blanket
a gravel road for namesake
a window guillotining fingers when it closes
fear-induced insomnia
the small hand of a Rolex
a lump under a lip
bed bugs lingering at the foot of the bed
whispered morse code
the first doctor note: insanity
mother's sympathy
instructions written on a mobius strip
a link stapled in construction paper
a black eye
$125/hour to talk
meds
other meds
a tea bag steeped too long

Boy

I was four the first time I stood before the open mouth
of guilt, stepping into my mother's closet,

the first time I stood frozen as a pillar of midnight,
wearing her black dress. A pillar of salt and woman,

hungry skin. I faced my burning
home. Not alone, a man's phantom limb

pressed heavy on my shoulder. So,
I locked the door to punch my way out,

and became blood-soaked fabric. And my home
kept burning, which is to say, the home was the mirror.

Or, I was the home and the flames were the mirror. Or,
I was the dress, or, I was a boy devastated, a mind on fire

as the door knocked. And silence entered the room
as thick as fabric.

Pulled From Water

(June 17, 2003
Richie Philips, a queer man, was found in Kentucky,
pulled from the river in a suitcase.)

If I wake
and my body is corked
like a fish sent away
to heaven remember me
a suitcase of koi
no arms or broken joints
rolling down the bottom of a river
skin bloated by hatred I am
a vision
      a miracle marked dead
        marked missing
        then found
surrounded by men and bloodhounds
I am alive
spitting out the bullet

Virginia

Careful walking down to the creek,
we've found bones in the cavern.
I, too, grow weary of hacking a lung
when I mean to apologize, but as we speak,
acidic water is slicing limestone

a mile beneath us. The asters smell
like concrete, the wind is louder
than a tower of falling coins, and no one
could have ever told me I would live
this long. To me, scotch is unbearable,

no thank you. We were talking politics?
Right, we weren't speaking. Don't you dare
call this sun-rot meadow beautiful.
Not after what it said about you.

Walk

Spiraling is just another fetish.
This black eye, another hickey.
The ice in the cocktail is melting,
and I check my heart rate.
I look into the hollow landscapes,
into the swell of bruising peach skin.
The ice is melting. The ice is thin.
There's a stalker beside the barstool.
There's a suture in the future.
There's the last call.
I trip over the barstool
and fall twice as far.
Muted by inches of flesh
and fat, a memory begins.
Down in the final, unleveled ring of gin
a needle scratches the circle and plays
a song I know. A song for a boy
crumbled like a house on fire.
The needle lifts and falls again.
It's now 6 am, the hour when hypothetical
conversations pour themselves through soup cans
connected by twine inside the head. The hour
of SUVs speeding towards the airport.
When highways are black-scaled snake backs.
The hour words move through the thimble
of the throat and become nauseous nothings.
Where cardinals fall second-guessingly
in all this dawn.

Listening to *Funeral* by Phoebe Bridgers, October 2019

I am home again, roommate screaming through the phone
at the nurse who stopped me from seeing a psychiatrist.
I search for a sleeping pill on the scratched hardwood floor.

I lay sideways like a dog in bed
and run my fingers over my chest, circling a lump
under my skin like a cruciform. I'm trying to posture myself
in forgiveness. I worry about the people watching me.

Later, I check my mailbox once more, just to leave
the room where the colors on the wall are vocal and panicked.

Marlboro 27's from the corner store, Anne Carson,
and a fold-out chair on the front lawn. I'm giving myself over,
perfectly still on the grass, eaten by wind.

Should it rain cold rain let something deep inside me grow.
Should it rain let the plates reassemble themselves,
let the twin of my body sleep well, rest ready.
Should it rain let me go inside and put away the laundry.

Identity Crisis

Hurry, put the marbles back in the bag.
You may be the only person born to this world

without an exit plan, leaving by chance.
You have so many unnamed phone numbers

written on corners of poems, on family recipes
and below the hardwood. Lay the hand flat

to feed a horse, lay the hand crescent
across your pillow, lovesick into the night.

There is no door to the basement because
there is no basement, but where is all that

noise coming from? You may be intelligent,
and have the answers, but you must

stop returning to the graveyard, beside the post office
and Knoxville's best barbecue, only to find

the megalodon mouth of polished tombstones and
a chorus of names you vaguely recognize—

a soup of spirits, a personal fiction you feel
you could have written under the correct circumstances,

and so you're moved by yourself, moved to leave
in fear of your own story, written by the twin of your body

we'll never really know.

When I Was Young I Confessed Every Single Thing I Ever Did

Twice over, maybe three. When I was younger I swallowed a quarter because I was learning about Hades. I can promise you one thing, they're coming to collect. Listen, once I left a candle burning and the dog home alone. Once I eyeballed my prescriptions too long and was fed by my roommate for a week. Once I looked when a friend was changing. Once I was drunk in church. I forgot that to be meek doesn't mean small. Once I swallowed something entirely unlike a coin but the taste was similar. Once I blocked someone, double-locked every door for a month. Once I came back home and the juniper trees erected the end of my 20's. Once I let the wrong twin win custody of my mind. Once I told one of my classmates that another student was gay after I slept with him. The same thing happened to me. Once I danced to Fleetwood Mac with the windows bared open to the street after they wheeled off the body of my neighbor, drunk on tiredness, freshly diagnosed. Once I messaged a guy from my street under a blanket during a party. Once a church boy kissed me in the name of fellowship. Once I came to on a bridge and drove home. Once I violated my cracked, huge heart. I don't think I meant harm. Twice I tried to pray again this year. Once I learn how to keep my mouth shut it's over for you fuckers.

Pitt Street

If I were God I would also start with light.
Wood, when petrified, looks more like stone
than some stones. I, when petrified, sing every
song that I know incorrectly, stitch names that I love

into *You Are My Sunshine.* I sing this because grief
never loses an argument. You pretend the wall
hasn't moved, like it isn't impossibly far from yesterday,
but I can't criticize how you choose to survive.

What I'm trying to say is if you hate
razor burn, there are a million ways to avoid it.
Have you ever cried while the blasting heat
wrote your face dry and the windows

were rolled down in December?
I cherish the fruit pit, no matter how unsurely
I identify it. If I told you this poem was written
from a bridge, I'd expect you to believe me.

I Told My Doctor, Father, and God

the same story. How I spoke
the devil back into existence,
how I followed the trail
of flies to find his named wrath.
Musk can be holy, musk can be
harmful before the smell
of liquor. This table
in the kitchen, where I write,
is gutted by fallen angels.
I promise you, to bare all
and to bear all are not
very different. There still is
grief in the garden,
poppy namelessness and total
unrepair right where you left
it, beside the blueberries.
I promise you, the life
I should have is coming.

Crying After Your Birthday Party

To stay is to consume
further. So you pull at the sleeve
of matches until one frees.
You pick at your teeth.
You pick at your teeth.
You pick   teeth.

Apricity

To stand in ruin, to stand center
of your own precious life,
like a clipped raven who whistles
as it flies, is a backward sentiment.
Somehow every phone call becomes
a poltergeist, numbered brackish voices
you've disarmed in cruelty, a phantom
bottle emptying itself into your blood.
It's a shame for both of us
that there is no speech surgery,
no way to enlarge the correct letters
in the correct order.

It's snowing.
Water the moon cannot touch.

Inside the Steeple

1.

Already at the age of seven
      I heard a lie.
I was building steeples, to celebrate,
      the marriage of my Batman and Robin.
They married. They kissed. My brother
      weighed boulders over my shoulder
and crushed the oasis. I remember. He said
      It's not real, that's fictional.

2.

Before then, a man. A grandfather.

 Before then, a man became a bludgeon,
hell-bent on teaching Gomorrah. Said,

 God said so. Said, feel my fearing. Said,
here is the way a body swells.

 He held my brother by the neck. *Which one?*
Your eye, your right eye will remember.

 Your right eye will feel the phantom monuments
of stones before you cross a river. It will

 remember God walked here first.

3.

I know you, lover, I know
     you are nonfiction. Somewhere. You are
complex carbon. A body equal, even if I don't know
     the weight of you yet. I know the wait weighs
a cathedral's worth. I am crystal-heavy
     with anticipation. I am failed in my guessing.
A name—what is yours?
     I turn my shoulder and look back.
I turn to salt.

4.

When I know you, when I know
       the edges of your name, will I
also know a torso ripe enough
       to touch? Can we then
walk around those
       picketing our way to heaven?

2.

Triage

"All I've Suffered, and all the suffering I've caused,
might have arisen from the lack of a little salt in my brain."
—Robert Lowell

Are you thinking of hurting yourself right now?

The oyster knows the safest place
to hide its pearl is inside the mouth.
If I show you, show you the violent
flashes of memory I've swallowed, you'll snap
me in half and take what I've nurtured.
Say the answer is "yes," or it was.
I know the lamb that bleats the loudest
is also the first to find the knife.

Have you thought about hurting yourself in the past?

Imagine a cardboard box,
burning at the edges. Imagine fitting
inside of it. Imagine the twin
owls nested in the corner of the porch
waiting for charred scraps to eat. So, this is
Sodom, so this is burning alive. To beat
the hell out of yourself. Yes, I've tried.

Are you on medication, have you been before?

I will swallow the small lunar pills
that shift the tides inside my body—
they're already inside me. See, I am
a painting of crashing seascapes.
The gulls are trying to make sense of the fighting
and the triumphed. I am a witness
to how easily an ocean can burn,
to the washed-up wildlife and sandcastles
lost as quickly as their memory.

Do you have a family history of mental illness?

How many hands have already touched me?

How often do you have panic attacks?

The temporary psychosis, the bloodfire.
A prairie of lost souls and men whose hanging
chains still rattle in the barn.
You're talking about the godwind
and the archers who never miss. I know
them, how they lift my dog
from his sleep when they enter
the house. Each one an unnamed color.

What do you think we can do for you?

I'll show you a new prairie, dyed red.
My dog with two heads. I'm Geryon, still
alive. Still a kaleidoscope of desire,
of ill wanting and invincibility. Listen,
to me with your stomach while mine
is still not yet gutted. Help,
my cattle are burning all they touch.

Redacted

I am writing with blood-wet
charcoal

in clothing
made from locust shells

   Listen, to the open window
that sounds like a bridge

to the still sliced fruit
empty of sound

I've lost my voice
   in the boys I love
who asked me to lay face down
in the street

not looking at the stars or stoplights

just to lay there

Litany of Summertime Forgetfulness

What is the word opposite of benevolent?
The body is an angry god, pulling back
the arrow. I forget birds have tongues.

The first time I cut down a tree I found lungs.
The first time I was cut there was a dogwood bloom
tucked under netted strings of muscle.

Remind me: the word that is used for the fear
of your own desire, or for counting
all the ways it will be used in anger against you.

Tenderizing? Velveting?

The bugs are biting. The bugs are gnawed
and flagging down help. Here
are the toadstools growing over a stump

of grief. I forget about cold water. I forget this
is what a heatwave feels like. This isn't a sunset.

It's the antihistamines dispersing as prescribed.
I forgot: what is the word for the attraction
to carnage, or, for the dangerous animals

that look just like you.

I Want to Be Loved

with all the bone matter evenly dispersed
between wet jaws. Loved like amber, like open
flame, like all things lost to deluge.
I lose myself, cup-handed, because we enter
naked and leave concussed. There is no better
word for *friction*, and still here I am
making chicken shit sing
like a drowning chorus across the page. Still,
at the tip of my tongue is frazzled thought, flavored
cherry, melting membrane. How imperfectly
we move through water, only—
I bless anything that falls from the sky, on my own terms.
Didn't I call this a cause for celebration?
To fall heart-first on the pissy concrete, like a doll
who never closes its eyes. And then
Dancing Queen plays at the bar, and the only ending
is a distant one, a lightyear or so depending
on your equipment. It burns so slowly,
and you drink so quickly, and all the blood
you swallowed out of embarrassment
reeks your breath, and you forget the current president,
and the date, and the time, and the date.

Symbiotic

You come to me flavored in verbal refrain, seasoned
like the mangled copper door hinge, the one door
leading to the well, beside the earth's hot edge.
Are you good and lost? Are you sniffing the Lapis Lazuli,
hoping for more purple? Stand dead center of the street
and let the tide carry you until you ache
for a bowl of rosewater, for the loving hearth. No,
you cannot go backward, never could.
I only have love in my heart for you.
Would you like a cigarette on the frosted lawn?
Nothing is ever answered by putting on
your most comfortable clothing. Still.
I'm your dirty little Armageddon, a beautiful blast
in blue khakis, the longest chin whisker
always begging for attention, but you have no
business listening in for this long.
Round the corner you'll find the way out.
Plant this in wet soil.

Monaco Drive

If I could choose my last word, it would be resurrection.
The bedbugs at the foot of the frame have chosen rust

instead of compromise. I kick up so much sand
that this planet reeks of ecru. Could you imagine

having so much confidence, the vodka shot
chokes back only laughter? There are a million ways

I could build a man, give him a name, a regular
shaving schedule, make him dress and undress—

but could you believe all the ways I've dressed myself
in suburbia? There's a glow in the passenger seat,

dust that never settles. Believe the worst part
of your imagination. The bar tab was small.

I paid it. If you follow me back,
I sleep with the bedroom door locked.

Mr. Imagination Pours Himself a Glass

I love your mind.

> Let the mind continue its discourse
> on drywall. Let a body heal. Hallowed light
> of hangover, I pray again for the miracle
> of evidence destroyed, skin restored.

I love everything that surrounds your mind.

> Call this place home. Call this place
> hell. Call this place when you shuffle
> through the park before dawn. Fathers
> always find salvation when their sons do.
> If you're looking for me, look beneath
> the asphalt revisions, where I'm making peace
> with the dogwoods.

I ask of you only what everyone else solicits:
> *peace,*
and a frame to fill.

> I left God another drunk voicemail.
> I prefer candlelight with my whiskey.
> Somewhere an evangelical is praying
> for the seventh seal to open. To bring
> heaven closer, and to move hell down.
> He asks this lightly.

I love you like anger, like a cold
> *front loves the lilies.*

> If I'm lying, then I've made you
> an object lesson.
> In the next life, tie a cord around me
> so I am not so easily lost.

Again

I follow his pointer finger as he pinches
the chem trail, pretends to unzip it. A new world,
where our bodies are not so small.

I want to carry warmth with me like that,
to radiate like vineyard stones into midnight.

But I'm here, blowing smoke on spiders,
watching planes fly over the unkempt lawn.
And he has a face only a sculptor could fashion.

I'm finally at a loss for words.

Go to a Museum

I have renamed
    my grief   *Body*
for how little   I understand it.
Cosmically speaking,
    I am an afterthought,
or, too small to be
    spoken to tenderly.
My own stomach   and blood
    call me by other
       names. Cosmically speaking,
I love him. But this
     is not a sex poem.

This is not a poem
        about how the body learns
    itself horizontally.
So what
if his frame
    is a sculpture? Go to a museum,
there are more.
        This isn't a sex poem,
this isn't about
    how I already call him
family behind   closed doors.
This isn't a poem.

This is
    Joy speaking to you
like a lover,
throwing small rocks   at your window,
writing down everything
it loves about you.
    I promise, Joy
is breathing,
    naming itself
in your mother's tongue. Joy
        is casting long shadows,
    not muddled by midnight, kissing
the asphalt with your shoes.
      Joy has named this year
progress and taken pictures.

Joy speaks
like the right kind   of family.
                    Joy,
let me tell you:

I love him.
I love him. Halleluj—
ah, I am sorry.

Highway

Me, already wrecked
in false expression, have you noticed
that?   & your reticent mouth
is already closed over every other name I've so far
forgotten. So I come for you:
pockets of gravel, suburban haze, littered
roadkill.   Forgive me, in misery
                    I let myself hope.
Keep pace,
          I want to make it out of here
alive.   I'll try to be
a bit more concrete: the ash
        wetting on your beer can.
The ash settled on our verbal meandering.
The morning light—a halo—yours.
I will try to be more
            concrete: the pastel glow
of a Nintendo 64 loading screen. 4 am,
again.   My mouth, already
blurred by liquor—yours.
Maybe I will try to be a bit
more concrete: there's a highway—
            between our lips.

Nocturnal Animals

In the middle draft of the night I fell whisper to
how your voice sounded like spring, so to say,
the phone died and we had no way home. I'm saying
downtown looks good on you, and I like the way you talk
to Uber drivers, the way you talk to my dog.
I like that you keep your cool in the wet speed of the night,
like an animal with polite instincts, wading over puddles
colored in the light of bars we can afford and restaurants
we cannot. If I had any more sense I'd probably look
closer to the hot lights of the city, but I'm distracted
looking at my wet shoes, taking an inventory of joy.

Eating Over the Trashcan

The world
is not a caretaker,
not ready to hold
all things falling. Not a lover,
ready to stroke our napes
during a migraine. No,
I'll give it all, instead,
to fleeting cocoa and sharp
fruit that thaws
on the tongue. Pleasure,
how it leaves us _____,
how it leaves. I want only
to slow dance like maple.
To be a citrus rind
and fill the room.

A Love Poem

I, like the world, sweat on this Monday night.
I park my car that smells like fresh pita. Valentine:

Patron Saint of to-go bags and single-use plastic.
My grandmother stands 60 yards away, waving patiently,

but I'm too sick trying to unread every omen to notice.
I'm fraught looking forward. I need more time,

and less inevitability. The bald spot on my Labrador—
spreading. I didn't slow, either, on the way when the opossum

wrenched into a grotesque blossom, beside the pothole,
fleecing the asphalt in maroon. I have no appetite.

I'm going to leave. Have I told you about the crows?
I've never known where to place them.

The two that fell into the gutter. I suppose that's why it's called
a crowbar. The first one flew away. Its world opened.

The second stayed. Its world opened? And have I told you
about the kid I used to know, or, how he became the guy

I ran into at the bar the other month, or how he once again
became the person I used to know. His obituary

was never published. And when I heard, I drove.
And I knew him before the pothole widened,

when I drove hours, tirelessly. Before I drove, I was driving.
I'm saying that in every before I was driving the black veins

of America. Though now I'm parked, standing inside
the world, in the guest lot at the retirement community.

And if I look up, I may be tempted to feel
so splayed open in melancholic February that

I cannot deny I am alive. How could this have ever been
a love poem? I'm trying to piece something together.

Sunday Scaries

Every bird with a voice has long left, every familiar pillar
of light pulled before and later. Didn't I tell you
of my love for the mountains? How gospel music rolls
down the cliffside like a geological event.
Surely some sign will follow. If this is the end,
or close to it, it was an honor to eat
everything this world had to offer,
to have said *hello* and done so little.

Cycle

You're trying to build spires out of joy
because you haven't lost everything that wounded you.
Don't believe me? Count.
You make listless things name themselves.

Because you haven't lost everything that wounded you,
you are rich beyond belief.
You make listless things name themselves,
what a perfect kind of power.

You are rich beyond belief.
Don't believe me? Count!
What a perfect kind of power:
to build spires out of joy.

Elegy for the Ghost in My Kitchen

I take the jacket from your shoulders and bring
a mug to your lips. Drink this tea, this gin,

this bleach. Let it clean the walls of your veins,
the growing masses knotting in your brain.

I ask what it's like to be an ant farm.
To have a body full of hunger.

I ask in circles so you'll stay longer.
And you slice your arm and show

the empty inside it. You slice
an orange because it's your favorite.

Drink and visit a while, stay
like you aren't already gone.

Eat the orange as if it didn't drop
when I tried to give it to you.

Like my dog isn't carrying it
in his mouth, wondering who I'm talking to.

Praise

Praise the long-lost phone number.
It's been sixteen years
and I still cannot find a metaphor

for loft beds. Too busy, looking
at the shoes standing outside
my bedroom door. I keep

the photograph of the succulent
in the middle drawer, a token to remember
how it feels to take a picture of a succulent.

You would be amazed how open
to the world you become alone
in your kitchen in the middle of the night.

To make bread, when you're hungry,
to make the kitchen smell like bread,
I've come to learn, is an act of god.

Outside the Ark

After Waterline by Ocean Vuong

Let's say it: we're drowning
in this urgent minute. the god-
hands, wringing out the water.
We are dead
center of the storm, surrounded
by the drumming of rain
and the smell of spores
lifted by sudden humidity.

Face it, our bodies are broken
and covered in each other's sweat.
Our bodies are covered
by the last embarrassing lock
of sunlight as it closes, and we
are closer to each other
than a shadow to skin.

How many times will we drown standing upright?

I don't regret loving you,
even under the thunder and cold.

Promise me, when it's done,
you'll know that the water
that buries us will remember
everything. Maybe bodies float
because the ocean is hungry
for something else. Maybe ours
will lift over the horizon like dawn.

First Crush

This time it's a man,
and he's building a garden,
and I am only watching
as close as a breath. But I'm learning
how to love his tough-skinned hands,
the hands faithful to their soil
and growing things named by heart.

The two of us, behind the high
wall of hedges
(Buxus Green Velvet) feels
like a secret. I'm still cynical
enough to call us cliché.

There's enough literature already
for the forbidden gardens,
and the lovers waiting
to be cast out by burning arm.

Even if this is forbidden, my eyes
are still drawn to his movement.
I'm still crooning for the foliage
(Walker's Low Catmint) and envying
the attention the flora (Achillea
Millefolium) receives from him.
I want what they have:
time spent under his eyes
and between his shoulders.

Gardener, I can speak now.
Gardner, speak clearly:

You (beloved) keep tending the ground,
and I (I) will (can now) admire (love)
it (you) openly.

Winter Prayer

Let my whiskey-loose tongue speak
well of itself. I have taken the hoof and paw-
beaten path. Funny, how calm it is
to die of exposure. Bring back your arm
of flame. Bring back light to the night sky.
Listen, I am only one more gulp
of cold water from never sleeping again,
and I don't have the heart
to tell my dog. I am reaching.
I only ask for one more spoon
of my mother's apple butter.

Sunday Morning Miracle

I sliced   a lime in half/

and found   my tongue already

      inside it.

Economy of Touch

After Cooper, age 8, yellow lab.

It all adds up to
I love you

I wish only for my stretched
legs or the soft tuft below

the drinking trees I shit
where I please and this

too is so you won't forget me
easily yes I saw you were crying

I only have one heart
listen I lose banquets to your open

hand I unfurl in the economy
of touch and love is more than this

but damn that feels nice
there's your answer my ass

says it all I'm happy
you're home

I am Always Going to Have These Feelings

Perhaps silence is best. I am always going
to have these feelings, like how the earth's fertile
scalp will birth a million colorful things,
despite some plants having a taste
for other life. The thick mark of my being
is laughable, the refrain is always dependent
on understanding, I hope you don't
understand what I'm saying. I hope
your morning started quietly. I hope the tea
didn't burn your tongue. I hope the mole
you've been worried about is a hollow intimidation.
I hope for only great superstition. I hope
the part of you that you've always wanted kissed
will be. I hope every color that this world presents
you with is a surprise. I hope you make peace
with your childhood home. I hope the water is clean,
I hope you drink deeply. I hope our longing
will become a prairie, eager and crowded with life.

Second Sunrise

Speak to me, for maybe the last
    time. This minute, already stolen,
turns away from us
      the same way birds
are turning from the city.
    Hold my hands
as if they are not
      already guillotines, as if this
kind of dying is not communal.
      So it does end in fire,
   in second
sunrise, and we will become
      the last great shadow, hungry.

Hurry, and hold your joy
      like it ever
knew you. I am so sorry
    that every word
I write is not an act
      of creation, but
the sirens are burning, they call
everyone to be a prophet, and ask we move
    off the crags into their drowning,
    they beg that we

listen. *Hold out your hands,*
    cup them,
   and see what you are given.

Acknowledgments

Poems from this collection will appear or have appeared in:

HAD — "Three Boys"

Wussy Magazine — "You Will Always/Never be Alone"

Rattle — "MEARCSTAPA"

Narrative and the "30 Below" Anthology — "Anthropocene"

The Crab Creek Review — "Boy" and "Triage"

Glass: A Journal of Poetry — "inside the Steeple"

South 85 — "Redacted"

Homology Lit — "Litany of Summertime Forgetfulness"

& Change — "I Want to be Loved"

The Florida Review — "Symbiotic" and "A Love Poem"

The Greensboro Review — "Monaco Drive"

Olney Magazine — "Go to a Museum"

Frozen Sea Poetry — "Highway"

Perhappened — "Eating Over the Trashcan" and "Winter Prayer"

"My Loves" Anthology with Ghost City Press — "Outside the Ark"

Stone of Madness Press — "Second Sunrise"

Many of these poems appeared in Stone Fruit, a chapbook published by Glass Poetry Press.

This collection took 6 years to write, many of which were difficult. I'm proud I wrote this collection, but so many people carried me while I did. I can never thank them enough, but I'd like to try it here.

Thank you to *Queer Family Workshop*, for giving these poems early love and giving me even more. You all changed my life, and my first memories of queer joy are with you.

Thank you to Peter, Bridgett, and Savannah, you were my very first readers and the first people to believe I could write, let alone write a book.

Thank you to my family, for not rolling your eyes when I told you this is what I want to do with my life. Thank you for being consistent, I know that's not always a given. Thank you for loving me.

Thank you to my former professors who nurtured me: Joy Harjo, Erin Elizabeth Smith, Emily Rosko, Gary Jackson, Jonathan Heinen, and Arthur Smith.

Thank you to the friends I don't have space to name. You know who you are. I'm here because of you.

Thank you, Josh, Alex, John, Zack, Haley, Sam, Ben, Christa, Connor, and Anna. You're the real ones.

Thank you to the other poets who've been a wise and loving sounding board: Jason B. Crawford, Taylor Byas, Joshua Garcia, Nicholas Goodly, Ashley Cline, Adam Gianforcaro, Alice Fulmer, and Georgia Moon.

Thank you to Halle Hill, for your priceless writing wisdom, your decade-plus friendship, and the belly laughs I still have not medically recovered from. If I can speak to anyone's character- it's yours.

Thank you, Mary Drake, for being my first lifelong friend, for loving me like a soulmate, and for answering the phone when I needed you. You're a gift I'll never return.

Thank you, Thirty West Publishing House, for giving this collection a perfect home with attentive care. You have a lifelong fan and a grateful author.

Finally, Andy, for loving me and showing me daily joy I never knew before. You changed everything, thank you.

About the Author

Gardner Dorton is poet writing at the foothills of the Smoky Mountains in Knoxville, TN. His poems have appeared in journals and anthologies like *Narrative*, *The Florida Review*, *Rattle*, *The Greensboro Review*, and elsewhere. His chapbook, *Stone Fruit,* was published by Glass Poetry Press in 2021. Gardner writes about queerness, bipolar disorder, and the South. Visit his website and say hello at www.gardnerdorton.com

About the Publisher

Follow Thirty West on:

Scan the QR code to visit our website:
www.thirtywestph.com

Milton Keynes UK
Ingram Content Group UK Ltd.
UKHW041352300924
1922UKWH00006B/10